Just like the stars

Clara joel

ISBN:

DEDICATION

I dedicate this book to God almighty and to my family for their support and encouragement.

CONTENTS

TO MY BRO DAVID MARK WHO INSPIRED ME

December 31-january 1

The sixth day of christmas is December 31st, the last day of the year. As if to remind us of what a rotten year it's been the weather is especially lousy. A cold rain have been falling for hours by the time i was ready to leave for the trip.

"Alison have you wore rain coat already?" asked mum from the kitchen.
"Yes mum," i replied holding my luggage behind me.

My dad was already outside waiting for me,even though i didnt like the idea, mum and dad insisted that i must go to my grand parent place, it was surpose to look like an holiday but it wasnt because holiday was almost over.

I walked gently toward the car with my

luggage, my dad collected my luggage from me and put it in the truck of the car. I opened the door of the car, Starring at the house,especially the spot where i usually sat down every afternoon to read.

"Always be a good girl, dont forget mum love you so much," my mum whispered, as she hug me.

My Mum was standing at the entrance of the door waving as the car went off, the car was on speed as we passed the highway, my dad didnt say anything to me and everywhere when i look through the window of the car seems bored to me. Not quite long i slept off not knowing when we got there.

"Alison! Wake up," my dad said. I opened my eyes and quickly look through the window, there were children playing at the front of a house painted in yellow and white, it was a big house, i came down from the car while dad took my luggage from the trunk and hand it over to me.

We walked passed the yellow and white house and walked toward a small duplex painted in orange and white, at the front of the duplex christmas light twinkle all around the house and two fifty-foot evergreens in the front yard, under the trees where stack giant brightly wrapped boxes.

"Dad are we there already," i said almost touching the evergreens.

"We are almost there,"he replied walking toward the entrance of the door.
"Now we're there," he said smiling.

Dad ring the intercom at the front yard entrance and the door opened, a young lady wearing a white apron was standing at the door smiling.

Wow, Alison welcome home," she said as she collected my luggage, i walked in starring at every corner of the sitting room.

The sitting room was well arrange but not as beautiful as the entrance of the house. The young lady gave us a glass cup of water and some fruit while we wait.
Not quite long my grandpa came in smiling he sat down on one of the chairs and then told the young lady to take my luggage to my already prepared room.

"Oh, Alison you've grown big, last time i saw you, you where a lot smaller," he said, as they both laugh, i didnt find it funny so i just chuckled.

"Whatever that is sitting over there i dont want to see her in this house," a young girl that look older than me said pointing at me as she walked into the sitting room.

"Sophine, this is your cousin, Alison she will be staying here with us as from now on," Grandpa said smiling again.

"Forget that Grandpa,"she snapped.

Dad was surprise as i was, he was just looking at her.
"This so called cousin is not staying here with us, period!" She shouted and slam the door.

I followed dad to the door when he was about to leave that afternoon, we hugged eachother, i waved good bye to him as he left. When i came back to the sitting room i saw Granpa still sitting down on the couch.

I walked closer to him and sat next to him where he was sitting.

"Alison, i want you to be careful around

sophine, that girl is dangerous," he said slowly.

I gasp but wasn't afraid, but when i remembered what happen last holiday, when i and my friend kate suggested we should go on a ride at the park which later turn out to be very dangerous, more like worst, that made me spend the rest of the holiday at the hospital, ever since then I've always hated the sound of dangerous Although its just a word.

I leaned forward.
"Okay, Grandpa," i said standing up.
I helped him stand up and watched him as he walked up the stairs.

The young lady that opened the door for us the first time we came in showed me my room. i took my bath and then sat down on my bed, as i was about to stand up, something walked out of from under my bed that got me so scared, i turned and almost scream but when i look closely it was a dog, a puppy, i bend down and carried it, i groom it with my hands as i walked down the stairs.

"Look who found a new friend," Grandma said smiling.
"Grandma!" I shouted with joy, and walked even more faster down the stairs.
"Careful, my daughter so you won't fall down,"she laughed.

I dropped the puppy and hug grandma, how much I've missed her, when i last saw her, it was on my birthday, after then i didn't see her again till now.

As i sat down beside her in the sitting room, she took a wrapped gift out of a box from beside the couch and hand it over to me.
"I didn't give you my christmas present for

last Christmas, we're starting a new year i figure that's worth celebrating,"
"Thanks, grandma," i said as i slips off the wrapping paper and lift the box lid. It took me a moment to realise what i was looking at, a purple diary and a small box of chocolate.
"That diary is for you to write down all the moment so you wont forget," Grandma said smiling.

2 THE STRANGER IN THE NIGHT
January 2

The next morning after brushing my teeth i took my bath wore my blue jean and turtleneck sweater. I could percieve the aroma of fried turkey when i was half way down the stairs, on my way to the dinning room i bumped into sophine i tried talking to her but got no reply.

Everyone sat quietly that morning as diana served the breakfast,after praying we started eating. Not quite long sophine entered the dinning room,she walked passed grandma and grandpa without greeting went into the kitchen, later she came out with a glass of fruit juice as she was about to leave grandpa called her.

"Sophine, are you not going to eat breakfast with us today," he asked.

Sophine eyes narrowed. "what did you

say?

"You heard me,"

"You turn my mum against me and screw out my visit to see her, and then what? You think I'm just gonna tag along and sit arround this table with this ," she hissed. " And pretend we're having a nice family breakfast? I'd rather drink gasoline,"

I've never seen grandpa so angry before as he was that morning, he stood up as if he wanted to smacked her, but I'm sure he was scared.

I spend the rest of the day in my bedroom its hardly quiet with sophine always playing the music, though it was private.

I tried reading but could not concentrate

with all that loud music playing, so i came down the stairs that evening i checked the time, it was almost time for night prayer, sophine had already turned off the television and everywhere was quiet now. Goodnews, my grand parents where already getting ready for the prayers and i was feeling even more bored like ever before.

After prayers that night i went to my room, put fluffy on the his bed. Fluffy thats the name of the dog i saw under my bed. Then i went to my bed and slept.

That night i had a nightmare, i woke up feeling scared, then i heard a sound from down the stairs, it was like someone was walking slowly and softly so no one would notice then the sound suddenly stopped, i gently came down from the bed and walked toward the door i opened it gently i huddle behind the door when i was halfway to the stairs, that was when i saw someone dressed completely in black that made him look almost invincible, i squeeze into the door way or crouch like a tight ball holding my breath until the person pass by. I saw the person passing through the window when it left the house, After some mintues i turned toward my room then bumped into something i screamed so loud that everybody sleeping woke up. Not knowning it was fluffy he had been there all this time and i didn't know, grandpa saw the broken glass on the floor and the window was opened too.

I told them what i saw but sophine doubted it , for the first time since i came to my grandparents house she have talked to me, everyone was scared but i wasnt i was determined to know who it was that entered the house that night. I started by plotting out my plans, i thought that i would stay up every night after evening prayers and then when i see the person i would scream, but that would be lame, because before my grandparents would come out of their room the person would have escape.

So it took me three weeks plotting my perfect plan, grandpa already instructed everyone to lock their door before going to bed Every night, the police investigation was lame too," Hmm i mean everything."

January 14

The fourteenth of january starts with about six inches of snow on the ground, by the time i was taking my morning breakfast, though the sun is starting to break through, and the icicles along our roofline are driping steadily.

I was surpose to go back home now since the holiday was over but my mum and dad suggested i should stay with my grandparents while i attend a new school i didnt like the idea because i was going to miss ivy, Alice and all our plans for this term.

Everything happened so fast i got enrolled in a new school a little bit far from the house, i was going to start today my mum already called me, to pray for me in the morning before breakfast. I wore my denin jacket, black jeans, over coat i already wore my glove and scarf and was ready to go.

The school bus was now already outside by the time i finished my breakfast, my grandma followed me to the door she hug me and i kissed her on the cheeks. My new school was a lot better than the old one, because all the equipment where available but it was almost obvious that the students dont like me.

My first day at chilton high was way worst than the rest of the days, wonder why? I walked down from the school bus just like every other teenager but i didn't know the class that was surpose to be mine, i walked through the hallway almost five times, just like every other schools i did attend my mum was always with me from the principal office i would have know my class, but this was different.

As i was about to ask one of the student a teacher walked toward where i was, she stared at me until i felt like i should speak

"I'm... I'm Alison brattle, A new student, I'm looking for my class," i stammered.

"Hmm," she muttered. "I've been watching you ever since you walked into this hallway,"

I grabbed my bag handle tight, i then

walked a little closer to her, all the student passing by where just staring at me.

"So it appears," she taps a sheet of paper." Tell me something how long have you been walking to and fro in this hallway?"

I pratically choke. "A few mintues,"

"Are we talking about time?" She promts." Two? Five?ten?"

I finally shrug. "yes ma,"

"Okay, just because you're new here I'm just going to pardon you, but i wont tolerate this from you again, if it happens again," she repeat snapping her glasses back on and reading from a book she was holding. "Alison thats you're class." She pointed a class at my front and then smile.

I turned in surprise, and then whisppeard to myself "what a fool."

"what did you say?" She asked.

"Nothing, miss." I replied.

She gave me a book and walked away. I walked into the class, and sat down according to the number wriiten on my welcome to school book which was nineteen my seat was at the middle of the class by my right was number twenty which was a girl with blond hair sitting over there, by left number eighteen, a boy who have been starring at me ever since i walked in, he then looked up and shouted.

"Everyone we have a new student over here!" he shouted.

The whole class burst into laughter except the girl by my right who was just looking at me, it was just like the class was full of weirdo.

"And thats nothing even though she is new here, we havent even know how stupid she can be," a girl from the back seat shouted.

"What do you mean?" A teacher said walking into the class. "You have been apprehended, Alissa everytime you've-he picked his words carefully-" cross the line."

The whole class was quiet now after i introduce myself to the class things change a lot, nobody was talking to me except Dawn the girl sitting at my right in the class.

After school that day i and Dawn walked home together but to our surprise Alissa and two other girls had been following us but i later realise that alissa live next door very close to my house, that sometimes i can even see what she's doing in her room when i open the curtain in my room.

"You need new clothes," she stressed. Picking up the sleeve of my denin jacket in her hand in a mock of disgust.

"This...this is a disgrace." She shook my hand, and i jerked it back. Feigning like i was hurt.

"What's wrong with my clothing?" I asked, stepping back from her.

 "Everything," she and the two other girl laughed.

And i rolled my eyes.
 "I dont think there is anything wrong with my clothes, okay." I said turning to leave.

 "I am comfortable, and i don't look terrible thats all that matters,"

"Really." She laughed out again. "You call this clothes, more like rags,"

"Alissa, just stop okay, its enough Alison didnt talk to you and you started blabbing about clothes, have you looked at yourself at the mirror, oh my gosh, you look like a mop," Dawn said as we walked pass her.

She kicked a stone on her way, about following us, watching it slowly stumble off.

4 MY MISSION BEGINS

The next morning. My grandma sat with me on the dinning table long enough to make sure i ate my breakfast. I set my time according to the clock over the stove- 7:51. Very careful, i wind the watch, hold it to my ear, and when i heard it ticking my heart skips a beat. I straps it on, and even though the watch band hang loosely on my wrist, the watch looks awesome.

I've never felt so mysterious in my life.

At 8:20, i was already inside the school bus, pull on my new gloves and zips up my winter coat, when we arrive at school that morning i was feeling even more cold.

"Alison, are you okay?" Dawn asked as we both walked into the hallway.

"Nothing, just feeling a little cold," i replied.

"Hmm ok,"

"Hey, what are you two doing?" A new voice perked in, and we both turned to kayla and josh.

"Hi," i said.

"So i guess we should get to class?" Kayla suggested.

"Yeah," said josh walking away toward the class.

"We all know- especially you, that you are going to have the highest classes," kayla said with an eye roll.

"Well you didnt have to say it, you ruined all my fun," dawned said, with a grin falling easily.

"Oh, sorry," replied kayla.

Immediately we saw one of the teacher walking toward where we was standing we pretendly walked into the class-room.
Another thing about this class; was that i

and dawn where the only girls. you wouldn't think would be hard, but i find myself blending more with my studies like Ever before. I thought they where going to judge me on how my hair was today. In some aspects the guys were a lot easier to get along with.

Class started like normal; the teacher mrs eleanor, droning on and on about part of speech, though it was boring. I know the school rules it was written on my welcome to school book, if we disobeyed any of the rules, the backs of ours hands might end up not being there anymore.

That feeling, when you notice that someone is starring at you the back of your head numbs. I sat frozen for a moment.

"Is everything alright, Alison brattle?" Mr eleanor broke my concentration on the guy's eyes, and i reacted quickly, reaching to the ground.

"Yeah, just dropped my pencil," i said picking and imaginary pencil up the ground, giving another glance at the guy. He was starring at the teacher with a blank expression again, i did the same.

After English class the bell rang for lunch time. I and dawn shuffled through the slowly moving line to get food at the snack bar.

"You know that guy that sit behind you in English class?" I asked dawn, pouring hot cheese into a styrofoam cup.

"Yeah," she said, snatching up a soft pretezel.

"What's his name?" i asked casually, not bothering to touch anything in the line.

She laughed. "You dont know his name." I gave her a confused look.

"That's justin blake, the most hand some and quiet boy in our class." She said punching in her code into the check out.

"Hmm..." Was all i responded, and we sat down beside the group. Kayla, josh, dawn and me.

"Alison, tell us about your crush," said josh snacking off some fries from the table.

"What..., What Crush." I pratically choke.

"Dont try to hid it, everyone saw the way

you guys were looking at each other in English class," replied josh.

"He looked at me first," i said resting my arm popped up, as i listened vaguely toward their conversation. Justin, who seemed to be Every where. Well except here, i didnt see him at lunch, i probably would've noticed. My stomach grumbled in complaint to the objection of the food, but i ignored it, i could eat better at home.

"Alison, aren't you eating...?" Dawn asked.
I sighed, "I'm not hungry..." I said pushing her hand away from dangling in front of my face,
"And anyway you know i hate spagetti and meat ball."

"So what classes do you have next?" Kayla asked, tearing her gaze away from josh long enough to acknowledge the two of us but the question was directed towards me.

"Nothing much, i have physis II and then chemistry, but i get sixth hour off," i grinned as their mouth fell open.

"How did you manage to get your class cut out?" Josh exclaimed, almost about ready to throw the box of french fries at my face in jealousy.

I shrugged, "I guess that's what you get when you happen to be super brillant like me,"

The bell rung again for the end of lunch and the three of them groaned as they walked toward the door with me. Off to physis II, and hopefully to see justin who seemed to shadow my every move.

After school that day i felt extremely tired to be walking straight out of school at the start, Dawn was with me, she's now my bestfriend we do almost everything together, my back pack was slung over my shoulder, it was full of home work, that seem almost endless, but i still got my mission well planned, i didnt even bother to tell dawn, because i thought it was family stuffs.

That night after prayers i walked up the stairs to my bed room just like every other days by the time i heard a sound down the stairs i was already dressed. Black jeans, black long johns, black sweater, black coat, black socks and black sneakers. From head to toe in black i look

<h1 style="text-align:center">like a black ninja!</h1>

I walked down the stairs quietly i could see the stranger in the kitchen packing some things into his bag i quickly hide at the back of the door and watched him leave through the same window he broke the last time, i followed him quietly everywhere was dark, i huddled behind the base of a burnt out street lamp and watch the stranger walked into the mist of soke guys with bags all dressed in black. I note where they park and which resturrant they entered. Despite the earlier snowfall, the day warmed up and now, even with puffs of wind coming off the bay the night is pretty mild. Dressed completely in black i feel pratically invisible, when i saw them coming, i squeeze into a doorway or crouch into a tight ball between parked car, holding my breath until they passed. Then i spring back in action. Slinking in the shadows, i work my way down the water front until i saw them stop, when they stopped i got an unpleasant surprise. That when i saw the stranger in full form, a tall, skinny guy. He walked closer. My impulse is to skip the place althogether. What if this guy sees me? Im sure dead meat. I'm not giving up so easily.

Squatting behind a mailbox across the street, i noticed that, he was holding a knife on his hand.

"Dont think i didnt see you!" He yelled into the night. "I saw you!" With two more steps, he'll round the corner and find me on the ground, so i tuck in my arms, roll under the suv and watch, breathless, as he steps into the very spot i had occupied two seconds before.

Keep walking! I pleaded silently. Please keep walking! But the shoes stop. Back up a step. Then to my horror, a knee lowers to the pavement. Then another. In the next split second, he'll look under the car, and my mission will be all over!

At that exact moment, one of the other man called him impatiently." jason, come on let's go do you want to get caught!" He spring to his feet and sprinting toward the parking lot entrance.

In a flash i roll out from my hiding place and scrambled up to a crouch. Like a black ninja duck. I waddle into the alley behind virro's and dash a full city block before i stagger up against a dumpster. As i gasp for breath, from where i was i saw them entered a house, inside my chest my heart is still beating so hard it actually aches i walked a little bit closer and peeked through i could see them clearly now they where three men and a girl.

"That's it!" I muttered. "my mission is complete, once i reach home, the following morning I'm telling grandpa everything including their hideout."

When i reached home i quickly change my clothes and wore my night clothing. I was dog-tired, i fall face first into my bed

5 THE CLOSE CALL

January 17-18

My eyes snapped open, and my room stood before me. I was lying in my bed. Blinking away the sleep in my eyes, i noticed my room was cold, i quickly stood up locating the source of the coldness, i noticed my bedroom window was wide open, the curtins blowing as the breeze drifted them further inside my room. Groaning i paddled over the window. Then i heard a knock at the door i quickly close the window and open the door.

"Alison, how are you doing?" Grandma asked walking into the room.

"I'm fine, good morning grandma," i greeted and kissed her.

"Come closer my darling," she said indicating a chair behind her with her hand, i sat on it feeling even more sleepy.

"Your mum called," she muttered.

"Mum called?"

"Yes," she began carefully.

"Ok what did she say?"

"She asked if your okay, and by the way, Alison dear, how is your new school,"

"Fine grandma," i replied. I glanced at the clock, noticing that i was late; i had to be at school in an hour. Cursing the alarm clock for not working for the umpteenth time.

"Oh... Oh my gosh I'm late," i shouted running into the bathroom, lingering in the waterfall of warmth a bit shorter than Normal; the chilled air still hadn't gone completely away in the room, i thought my grandma would have noticed, but she didn't. When i came out of the bathroom grandma had already arrange the clothes i was to wear.

"Thanks, Grandma, you even know what i like." I said giving grandma a kiss on her cheeks. I picked up the blue jeans skirt, green turtle neck sweater and sneakers.

"Don't worry about your breakfast diana will bring it up to your bedroom." Grandma said. Holding fluffy, who was still fast asleep.

My dark brown hair was pulled back from my face, leaving my eyes to lay back a little in the expanse of it. I had never been short, always on the tall side, my belt kept my jeans from sliding off my hips. I had long gotten sick of having to pull them up every three seconds, and went through the uncomfortable of wearing a bulk belt, but atleast i wasn't always having to discreetly yank my jeans back up. Grandma gave me my back pack and we walked together down the stairs. but i was a little bit faster than her. I couldnt wait for diana to bring my breakfast, i walked into the kitchen, i looked toward the driveway but the school bus was not there.

"Diana, my school bus, did they...diana didnt allow me to finish what i was saying.

"Your school bus." She chuckled. " they came i told them your not yet ready so they left."

"Oh, my God, how am i suppose to go to school today?" I grabbed a mug out of the cupboard, Diana poured coffee on the mug i took some sandwich. And walked to the sitting- room. I checked my watch, and figured out i had a few minutes before i would have to start up the car. Actually i thought my grand parents where going to allow me to take one of the cars, but they didnt allow me instead they told sophine to drive me off to school.

After i finshed my sandwich and coffee, i threw the mug in the sink and went outside grandma was already there with fluffy. I kissed fluffy and pat him on the head.

"where did she put the keys ?" Sophine hissed walking toward the garage, she pressed the garage door opener. When diana finally brought the keys she snapped it from her hand and hissed. we got into the car and she drove off.

As she drove down the street, i tried to make myself remember the name of one of the stranger. I tried to remember the house i saw them walked into.

"Alison, get it to get it together, " i scoffed as, she pulled into the high school parking lot. Cars were already filling up the small parking Area, she managed to snatch a decent spot that wasn't too far away from the door. Slipping out of the car with a smile on my face but a liitle worried, she didn't even bother to talk to me, instead she threw the keys at me i catched it and immmediately she walked away.

I put the keys into my school bag and walked into the hallway, when i entered the class mr james was already in the class.

"I'm sorry," i said as i walked to my seat. Mr james drawled, slightly more animate than yesterday, but at least the students were pratically buzzing in their seats, as if the excitement of knowing this year assignment was too much.

There was chattering behind me, and i quickly glanced my eyes skimming over toward where justin usually sit down but wasnt there. A guy next to me, passed me a packet apart from the rest i looked over the list, and soon got caught up on the excitement that had passed over the room; the projects we were making were not easy in the least. A dresser would be taking up most of the marking period and i read through the schedule, all the student have been group in four each. Pratically ignoring the whole overview mr james was giving to the class on this year's project, i turned over to the next page, what i saw made me angry, Alissa, wilson, justin and i where in the same group.

The bell came on all to soon for me, and i collected my backpack, which was steadily filling with textbooks from various classes, and papers that where collected in them. We filed out of the room, everyone eager to get to lunch, the time where you could always count on knowing atleast one familar face.

I stuffed the book bag into the locker of mine with all my might, struggling to close the door with both hands pressed tightly aganist the metal, and my feet slowly sliding down the linoleum floor in a flash another hand appeared and the locker clicked as they gave a little effort to close the stupid contraption. I whirled around to see my helper, but locked on the steely eyes.

" oh, hmn thank you." I murmured reality crashing down on me.

Justin smirked. " Hello, Alison." His voice was calm.

" yeah." I said walking away he ran toward me.

"Can we eat lunch together?' He stated simply and indicated with a nod of his head toward the lunch room.

"No, my friends are waiting for me I'm eating lunch with them as usual," i replied walking toward the lunch line.

"We need to talk." He said as he walked into the lunch room. The noise seemed to be dulled in the croweded lunch room today, and giving a glance outside i noticed that it was raining, So glad we drove here.

"About?" I inquired walking towards the lunch line, that was moving slower than normal, not caring if he followed or not, but he did.

"Our project," he murmured, i could feel his presence behind me, sensing the fact that he was taller than me, his body radiated heat and i felt like snuggling up closer to him in the cold of the cafeteria the thought had me taking a steo further down the line, away from him, my cheeks blushing furiously as i snatched up a plate of whatever they were serving not bothering to check.

"I know, i saw your name as part of the people in my group, but we where four so where are the rest?" I asked.

We settled ourselves in the table of the farthest corner, i look to check, if my friends where sitting at our usual spot, thats was when i realised that each student where sitting according to their group members. It was close to the window as the rain pelted the side walk outside, making everything turn a darker color than before. No one sat arround this corner, preferring to stay closer to the other side, looking at the passing cars and such;

He was starring at me, his tray as untouched as mine was at the moment, but left my gaze on the fork, acting as if it had a sudden draw towards me, he sighed heavily, before running a hand through his black hair, making it stand up on end further before slowly settling back down into its gentle curls.

"I really dont know where to start," he chuckled nervously.

I smirked, still not looking up fully, toying with the napkin now.

"Mr james hasn't told us yet, what we are going to do," he said slowly, "we Alissa and wilson feel less concerned on this project," he said.

"Birds... Of the same feathers," i said sarcastically, finally taking one bread that resembled rolled up pancakes filled with cheese and dunking it in a cup of strawberry jam.

"Of course they are..." He scoffed with a roll of his eyes.

"So what are going to do about this project?" I said, taking a bite of the cheese stick.

"I dont know, but atleast we are the only one serious with this poject in our group," he said with a small smile.

I smiled a little, but went along with my lunch, thats when he started eating.

"Can we get to know each other," he said with a mouthful.

I raised an eyebrow as the conversation continued. We talked about all the aspect of our life, just the basics on my part; i wasn't going to tell him anything that might give myself away. He seemed pleasant to know. I had found myself actually enjoying his part of the story, no matter how few it was, but his words were drawing me in.

All too i found the bell ringing, and me with an empty tray; one of the first ive had since i came to school. Sighing, i guess i wouldn't eat as much for dinner tonight.

We got up and dumped the remainats of our meal into the trash can before walking out together to hallways.

6 THE BAD NEWS

Justin paused by my locker, and eventually help me pry open it, as it refused to succumb to a person who had stuffed it so full, then finally it opened and i took my backpack, he close the locker, shrugged and walked me to class. It wasnt a comfortable accompaniment, i felt nervous on edge arround him definitely not like a boyfriend walking his girlfriend to class. Thats probably what it looked like, but i would never date someone like him, i scoffed at the thought.

He gave me an amused look, as if trying to guess my thoughts but i just shook my head.

"Let's talk to wilson and alissa after school about the project," i sneered as we got to the chemistry II door.

He laughed. "Oh, you're right, i'll be seeing you after school,"

He started walking away, leaving me with my eyebrows scrunched together.

"Ok," i said about to open the door.

"Bye... His chuckle echoed off the hall.

"Great," i muttered, pushing into the class. The teacher gave a glance in my direction, before indicating for me to sit down.

"You're lucky its the second day of school this week, and if I'm still lenient, Alison brattle, dont be late again," mr fred said, as i slumped in my seat.

"You're grumbling a lot more than usual," Dawn commented as i walked up to her sixth hours, we were walking slower than normal not afriad that she would be marked late.

"I'm not," i countered, but i noticed the grumble in my tone and huffed, i wouldn't be walking next to dawn right now i could just go home, but i knew that justin was probably waiting for me.

Dawn gave me a pointed look, her eyebrow arched precariously, daring me to lie more to her.

"I'm talking about justin...," she said.

"Nothing, we are just talking about the project thats all," i reminded her.

"Okay, well i guess we will be seeing tomorrow," she said, and i smiled giving her a wave before she trottled off to her classroom.even though i felt a start of love growing toward go ol' justin, i felt determined to keep it a secret. I walked to the entrance of the school, feeling childish i pressed my face against the cool glass, to see the rain splattering hard against the side walk still, and the car only a short distance away. I was once again grateful that had sophine thought of getting a close parking spot today. I didnt see anybody outside, maybe justin had forgot about me? Smiling wryly, my phone started ringing, even though, we where not allow to take our phone to class my phone was always with me.

I picked the call and then listen, it was diana voice i heard crying.

"Miss, Diana, what's wrong, why are you crying," i asked feeling worried.

"Alison, your grandpa slumped this morning on the dinning table and hit his head on the table, they have taken him to the hospital just now," Diana said, anxiously.

"What!" I said almost in tears, "what hospital was he taken to?"

"Saint... That was when the call ended. I pushed open the door and rushed out into the cold rain. I was soaked to the bone by the time i had reached the car i dug the keys out of my pocket crawing into the car, i quickly fired the car to life with shaking hands. Turning the heat up all the way, i waited comfortably while the car's heating system was warming the car up. I leaned back in my chair, closing my eyes lightly. Sighing as the heat warmed my skin, the fact that i wasn't cold anymore.

There was a rap on the door, and i jolted forward, my eyes snapping open, my head collided with the sun visor that had apparently fallen down again, but i quickly looked toward's the passenger's side. A figure stood in front of the window, the figure meshed together by the rain, but they were obviously indicating that i rolled down the window.

I rolled it down, careful of the rain that was now blowing inside the car, trying to see who it was, a face appeared clearer, and i gasped, starting to roll the window back again quickly. but justin's hand shot forward stopping the window from closing, he pressed the unlock button on the door and was climbing into the passenger's seat.

I looked at him, as he shut the door firmly behind him, the window finally rolling up, a mintue too late for it purpose. He shook some of the water droplets off his hair, a simle on his face as he firmly turned to look at me.

"Alison, you thought i wasnt going to come out right, ive been watching you since." He laughed, and i found myself captured by his tone.

"What's wrong, you seem like you're not happy." He asked his whole face looking worried as mine. His eyes held mine and i found myself starring into his eyes almost in a trance. i snorted in disgust at myself and lost contact as i looked away, toward the window.

"My grandpa is in the hospital they said he slumped this morning, and went unconcious," i said almost in tears.

"Oh, sorry," he said reaching over, and unbluckling my seat buckle swiftl before i had the chance to drop my jaws.

"Let me drive you home, your not in a shape to drive yourself home," he said.

"No, I'm okay," i replied insisting.

We stay silent for a few minutes, it was very uncomfortable silence, but i cleared my throat and shook my head.

"Let me drive you..." He growled reaching over to the keys. He snatched them jingling ring of keys from his other hand.

"But it's just so fun... And you are so gullible," he snickered, and growled under my breath.

7 THE RETURN WITH SADNESS

January 18_19

The heat started to seep away from my body as the car's hot air was leaving through the vents. I stopped trying to grab the keys, and grasped my forearm to contain shivers that were starting to erupt on my skin, Justin's hand on my shoulder was hot to the touch like ember on fire, and i found myself leaning into his hold, to be wrapped in those warm arms.

He hadn't seemed to notice my likeness to his touch, but my coldness.

"Well seems you have a choice... You can either let me drive so you get the car warm again or you can deal with the alternative and walk home while i keep your keys for you," he shook the keys to accent the deal, i glance from him to the keys debating whether i would be fast enough to catch it by surprise. Probably not.

"Fine," i said sharply and he grinned, and waved his hand for me to get out. I winced, before crawing over to the passenger seat. He came in the driver seat just as i was snapping the seat buckle again, a look of worried was sure on my face i wasn't happy because of my grandfather illness. He smirked again, before hesitating to turn the car on again.

"I don't know the direction of your house will you show me?" He asked

"Yes," i said and he smiled. I glanced over at justin, his eyes was nonchalantly gived on the road, i noticed the way the rain drops had made his hair wet and curled in smaller, tighter curls than dry its black strands going even darker at moisture.

When we got home diana was standing at the door, she got into the car and justin drove us off to the hospital.Grandma was sitting in casuality crying i sat beside her while justin and diana stood beside us. We waited for about one mintues before the door came to see us.

"How is he?" Grandma asked in tears.

"Stable, we think he had a stroke, a mild stroke, we'd like to keep him here for a while under observation. We'll do some test all being well he can go home, in a couple of weeks or so, he will need a bit of looking after, because he had an amnesia and may not even remember anything, but we promise to do our best." The doctor said about leaving us.

"Can we see him." Grandma asked

"The nurse will show you the way," the doctor replied as he walked down the corridor.

My grand father was lying in a bed surrounded by array of monitors and drips there was a tube in his nose and another in his arm. His hair was gold against the white of the pilliow. There was a wide strip of. plaster across his fore head, and a dark grey bruise round his eyes. He was asleep breathing deeply, regularly, his eyes was opened.

"Who are you," he murmured as Grandma sat closer to him, i was standing beside Grandma while diana ans justin where on the other side. I looked at grandpa he was frightened, and agitated too.

"Its me, your wife you had an accident, you're in a hospital," grandma cried holding his hand.

"Its alright." I said helping grandma stand up while diana assisted her to the car. And justin followed them. I was alone with grandpa now i sat beside him, holding his hand i noticed it was cold.

" Grandpa, please get well soon," i cried watching his eyes closing slowly

"Don't worry, he will get better soon," justin said, slowly. That was when i noticed he was standing beside me.

The rain didn't stop, everyone sat quietly in the car until we got home that day, we went out of the car, heading inside the house, Diana assisted grandma to her room, justin sat down on the couch in the sitting room, while i walked up the stairs to my room. When i came down the stairs after some minutes justin was no longer sitting on the couch again, i peeped through the window i saw him sitting on the swing, his black hair curling in a wilt that looked natural.

"What are you doing out here, in the rain," I asked, as i walked toward where he was sitting.

"Nothing, just feel like, staying here ," he scoffed.

"See you are already feeling cold," i said

"How do you know?" He smiled wildly.

"Because I've been watching you, since through there?" I replied, with my hand indicating my window upstairs.

He smiled again, cleared his throat covering it up as a faint cough.

"Let's go inside," i murmured

"Oh... Its fine, i choose to sit here anyway," he stammered out.

"Come, lets go inside," i insisted. As we walked toward the door.

The fire crackled from the living room next to the kitchen, soft music played on the stereo system. Wonder why diana turned on the music, it was grandma favourite song that was playing.

"Wow, such soft music, i love them," he smiled. He looked me in the eyes, his warm eyes shinning as he smiled.I smiled back; As i watched him took off his boots and carefully placed them by the door, before he walked into the living room.

"Sit down," i gestured over to the set of chairs that was in the living room he sat down, i went to the kitchen to meet diana, she left me in the kitchen as i poured some hot tea from the kettle to the mug. I went into the living room gave the mug to justin.

"Thanks," he said trying to blow the hot tea.

"Will you stay for dinner?" I asked as i checked my cellphone instinctively.

"sure!" He replied.

January 20 - 21

The sky redden as the sun sets, bringing a new day, due to grandpa illness everyone have been having a hard times, especially me, school have been lousy to me, with so much work, assignment and even our project was just next week, worst of all my class was having test today.

My hand hung limply on the desk in front of me, holding a pencil that was tapping nervously against it, that was even getting on my own nerves. The test was sure to be handed out in the next few mintues was one that i have forgotten, totally out of mind. So now i sat here, a sitting duck, waiting for the test to spear me and set my grades plummenting.

"Do you mind, I'm trying not to freak out from this test?" Chloe, the girl in the front seat said in a friendly way, before going up to the teacher to ask to go to the bathroom. I gave her a smile that she returned as she walked out of the door.

"Today's test..." The teacher started standing up, and immediately i turned out of the conservation that had been happening a lot lately. My mind just thinking about grandpa and a lot of things, what class was i even in? I scrambled for an answer at the momentary mind blank, before glancing at the board mostly consisted of numbers and formula and i quickly deduced i was in chemistry class, great!

"I'll hand the test out, after i take a roll," mr fred said sitting back down in the front of his laptop once more in the past three weeks of school i had both crept and rushed toward now; my nervousness over nothing in particular was driving me crazy like mad. I was always on the edge.

"Chloe isn't here." The teacher commented, and i looked back toward him, his glasses were pushed slightly down the bridge of his nose, his gaze was landing on chloe temporarily empty desk.

"She's here, just went to the bathroom," i commented starting to tap lightly with my pencil again.

"I don't see her," mr fred defended.
"I just told you... You even allow her go the bathroom..." I started, my eye brows knitting in confusion. That was when i felt a little tap on my shoulder.

"He's just making a joke," dawn whisppeared in my ear, i noticed the slight smirk on mr fred's lips.

My cheeks tinted rough slightly, as i noticed my mistake.

"I...i knew that," i said, with a force chuckle. Dawn just rolled her eyes, and leaned back in her seat.

"Sure you did," she said.

I sighed, as the test landed on my table in front of me, a white dead letter that just needed my name on it.

After school i was actually getting out of the class as the same time as the others, having made a deal with mr fred to take the test sixth hours.

"Hey... Alison wait up!" Someone called from behind me, and i whirled arround to see dawn maneuvering through the hall in an attempt to get me, i stood idle by the door way waiting calmly, my mind pausing to wonder why she was so hysterical about making me wait. She caught up to me with a smile.

"Did you forget already?" She asked.

My eyes brows scrunched in comfusion, trying to scrounge up some reason for forgetting whatever she was talking about.

"Maybe..." I said slowly, and got me a well deserved eye-roll.

"You..." She said grabbing my hand fierely.

"Are you coming with me, to help me Set up for the party tomorrow, " she enunciated, it new to me that she was talking about it at lunch; could it really be tomorrow?

"I..." I started as she pulled me out the door into the reasonably warm sunlight. My eyes landed on my car in the distance, seeing me being pulled toward her red convertible.

"No but's, you promised to help, and you are, its not like you have anything better to do," she pointed out and even though i was worried she didn't noticed that.

"Its not that, my grandma is at home all alone with diana she need me now more than before," i said

"You told me before," Dawn agreed, "But i really need your help."

"I know you well enough that you'll be wanting for me to sleep over to spend the night," her head bobbed in agreement, and i grinned genuinely.

9 FAR THINKING

Pulling into the drive way, i blinked as a different car stood in driveway. its silver paint job was bright and shiny, the model looking on the newer range of things. Hesistantly i stepped out of the car, making sure the keys were firmly placed in my pocket. With a grin i rushed to the door, and flung it open, the sweet smell of dinner already being made drifting towards me as i walked up the stairs after taking my bath and now wearing a new clothes. I walked to the kitchen i took a apple while watching diana stir the stew.

"Where is grandma?" I asked taking a bite off the apple.

"She is on the other side a little far from here." Diana replied, as she add spices to the stew.

"What is she doing there?" I asked with a mouthful.

"I dont know! "

"Okay," i chuckled as i walked out of the kitchen toward where diana told me that my grandma was. When i got there i saw grandma standing by the river side looking at the stepping stones as if she was trying to look for a particular stone, there was the round unsteady stone, the pointed one, the flat one in the middle, there was a safe stone, where you can stand and look around, that was where she was standing, the next wasn't so safe for when the river was full the water flow over it and even when it showed dry it was slippery. But after that it was safe.

"Long time ago, i and your grand father usually stand or sometimes sit over here it was such a good moment for us," grandma mumbles shaking her head, from a corner of her eyes, a tear rolls down her cheek. I pull an handkerchief from my pocket and gave it to her watching her dried her cheeks with it.

"All those memories, of him makes me cry that he is lying down in that hospital

bed and i can't do anything about it,"
Grandma said in a voice that's dreamy
and disconnected, she open her mouth,
but no words came out. Instead it was
tears, from her eyes.

"No, don't say that grandma, you are
trying your best we are all trying our best
by praying for him." I blurted out. But the
look on her face is one of a pure heart
break. She barely whispeard.

"Everything will be alright very soon,
grandma trust God, he will always hear
our prayers because we our trust in him,"
i said as i assisted grandma to the house.

I slipped on my coat, and walked out
the door; the moment i started the car,
my phone started blaring with my
favourite ringtone, groaning at the

number, i debated whether to answer or not, in fear of being chewed out.

"Hello, Dawn?" I asked blandly, backing up of the driveway.

"Where are you?" She screeched in my ear, causing me to pull the cellphone away from me.

"Sorry... I had to look over my grandma when i got hone, she wasnt in so i went to meet her by the river side," i explained.

"Oh... She said softly, " you dont have to come over... If she is not feeling better, and need your presence," she said, sounding slightly disappointed.

"No, she is asleep now, and by the way diana is there to take care of her if she need anything," i replied.

She didn't answer me first knowing that i always feel hurt anytime i leave her all alone and when she need me I'm not always there.

"Well hurry, i guess, we have to start with those cookies," i rolled my at her persistence.

"Yeah, I'll be there soon enough,"

I snapped my phone shut, as darkness was falling over the car. The air didn't chill and my window was still left open, the breeze not as comforting as before, but still cool to the touch, as i think about a lot of things humming to the music playing.

Pulling into Dawn's parent driveway was

like pulling into my grandparents garage, it was just like my grandparents house.

The light were on in the doorway, and i could see Dawn's peering reflection in the window, i could picture her face pressed up against the glass. Laughing i parked my car and skipped up the side walk; mostly for her enjoyment, i could hear her laughs through the wall as i opened the door.

"What are you, in Game shakers?" She laughed.

"Because, Because, Because, Because!" I sang, throwning my hands up in the air
"Because of the wonderful games they create!" We chorused together before wrapping each other in an intense bear

hug.

10 THE SECRET MEETING

January 24- february 1

We walked into the kitchen where everything was laid out for cookies, and other types of sweets in the works. A kitchen apron was laid out for me on the counter, and i tied the strings of it behind my back, liking the fact how we both looked, like old women of fifties cooking in their kitchens. But the kitchen was far beautiful from the type you'd find in the fifties. The whole house was huge, Dawn's parents both being rich, plus her father being the CEO of a major company near-bye.

I pulled myself so i was sitting on the marble counter- top, my feet swining against the wooden cupboards below me. Dawn started pulling out more perishable ingredients from the seemingly endless fridge.

"We have so much cooking to do..." She tisked.

"We've done it before, i and my mum, on my birthday last year, but then we had some of my mum's friends to help us out," i said we a shrug.

"Really, but we are the only one here, i told josh and kayla to help me, but they are not here," she pointed out, shutting the fridge door with her foot, i hopped down, realizing that they weren't here; the two lovebirds were probably out on a date now, again.

"Well then we better get started without them," i grinned, eating a piece of the premade sugar dough, she swatted my hand away playfully.

"Yes, we must," she laughed.

That day after helping Dawn with the preparation for the party, pulling into the driveway, i saw my dad's car stood in the driveway.

I stepped out of the car, making sure the keys were furmly placed in my pocket, it was quiet around the house, like normal, but there seemed something off. I rushed to the door, and flung it open, the sweet smell if dinner already being made drifting toward me.

"Dad...?" I called out, and i saw my mum head pop out from around the corner from the kitchen.

"Alison... I was expecting you sooner, diana told me you went to help a friend prepare for a party," she chirped, her warm familar voice had me running into her arms. Instantly her arms wrapped around me, holding me close and i inhaled her scent; a soft mixture of her favoutirte cologne.

"Sorry mum, i had to stay to help her do some decoration," i murmured into her sweater.

"Hope you like your new school?"
She pulled back at me skeptically, and eye brow raised peculiarly high.

"Yes, mum, i even find myself serious with my studies like ever before," i grinned sheeply. She chuckled, as i kiss her on the cheeks.

"Best mum in the world," i whispered as i watched her laughed.

Sliding into the seat with an easy smile, i tried Peering over her shoulder to see whats for dinner.

"Mum, where is Dad?" I asked standing up from my seat.

"He is in grandma's room," she replied taking a sip out of the hot tea.

I walked up the stairs toward grandma's room that's when i overheard grandma and my father conversation.

"Won't that be too hard for her to bear,"

"I know, but with your father's condition we can't afford the stress,"

"Don't worry i will talk to her."

"Okay,"

"But can she stay here, while i pay for her school fees through the school account,"

"I was suggesting she should go back and live with you,"

"I sure know... Alison wont like this idea it was her dream to study at chilton high, before going to college,"

That was when i gently walked down the stairs, back to the kitchen sliding back into the seat and not smiling this time but a little worried.

"Alison," mum said nonchalantly, as she noticed i wasn't smiling like before.

"Did you see your father, did he say anything to you?"

My heart thudded in my chest, as i realise that i couldn't tell her what i overheard grandma and my dad saying, like, i'd always had, this time i was worried i had alot going through my mind. Taking a long drink of ice-tea that was set in front of me, trying to swallow away the words that i wanted to say.

Yes mum, I'm fine, its just that I'm tired," i said totally lying.

She gave me a sympathetic look as she sat down, setting two plates of macroni in front of us. I told her all about the classes i was taking my grades weren't surprising to her, i had always been the one to keep on top of them, maintaining them at steady "A"

My plate was licked clean, the remnants of red sauce gone as i scraped my fork against the plate in effort to pick up the microscopic cheese particles that tasted so good. She laughed

"I know you missed them, they are always your favourite, she chuckled,

and i laughed.

"There is more in the fridge for you later," i started to say thank you but caught on the word in the sentence.

"Me? Thanks mum," i said as i dumped my plate in the dishwasher.

Since today is friday, i was already thinking about dawn's party, like the dress i planned on wearing tomorrow for the party; that was when my mum brought a new dress to my room even though the dress look small, i only apreciated her for the dress, it was pink and black a beautiful designed but it look small and short.

"Alison, i bought this dress for you, i thought since pink is your favourite colour, maybe you will like this one," mum said, as she sat down on the bed.

"Thanks mum," i replied. I held it up in the air so the bottom half fell down to my knee height.

"You look so pretty on it," she said.

"But mum, i haven't even put it on," i murmured and she laughed

11 FRIENDLY PARTY

Unzipping the back of the dress, i stepped into it, waiting as i pulled it up for the moment where it would catch on my hips and threaten to tear. But to my surprise it felt snug arround them, but then tugged loose, coming higher, to point where i could place the strap over my shoulders.

I opened my eyes, not realizing they had been closed, and peered into the mirror, i frowned when i realized, dawn was already in the sitting-room waiting for me. Dawn sang from the stairs to my bedroom.

Her eye widened to the size of a saucer and an ear spliting squeal left her lips. I grimaced, as she ran toward me jumping up and down with the energy of a toddler.

"Alison, you look so pretty," she said in a high pitch voice.

"Really?" I asked, the feeling of a breeze traveling up my thighs was foreign and i was enjoying the feeling. She just grinned like a maniac.

"Yes," she said shaking her head frantically. "Alison this looks amazing on you, I'm not going to have you deny yourself one day of looking like the princess that you appears to under all that sweat shirt and jeans,"

Glancing in the floor length mirror, i saw that the dress did have a nice touch to it so i didn't feel as if i was dressing like a slut, and the straps atleast three fingers width.

"Thanks, Dawn."

She jumped up and down again, this time making her way around in a small circle.

"Yes... Now we get to do your make- up and hair,"

"No!" I said firmly. "My hair is fine as it is," i fingered through my hair, its straight strands only reaching to my chin, framing my face, it sun stained highlight were the only things i was proud about it.

She complained and tugged over to the vanity plopping me down in a small bench. The sound of the curling iron being turned on was like a warning sign to get out. But my hand was placed firmly on my shoulders,

"Let me have my fun,"

Somehow Dawn and her parents picked the perfect weekend to have the party it was warm the sun is beating down gently on the backyard area like summer, the backyard mostly consisted of a large running area, which had been decorated with various tents and bales of hay, some even set up in a formation of a soccer game. The pool had been opened for its final visitation of the year, the large patio surrounding it accompanied by coolers and tables of food that have been prepared for the party. Since their house was one of the bigger ones, they got their own private property, with a ridiculously long driveway.

"Oh, alison stop fussing, you look fine." Dawn said to me, as i furiously tried to tame the wild me that had become of my hair. It had been curled and sprayed, so it was now permed bunch resting on my neck. Apprently it had just passed Dawn test, so it must have looked alright, but i still couldn't help at the feeling weirded out by the back of my neck being bare.

"We still have another half hour," she murmured, as the dishes was set on the patio, careful in our shoes not to fall face first into the pool, which would surely put all her work on our appearances to failure.

"Hey A&D?" Someone called from the front of the door, and we both walked swiftly back inside to see kayla and Josh come in hand in hand. A pang hit my stomach faintly at seeing their hands clasped in eachothers, and i glanced over to kayla who was completely in tune to josh guess they wasn't totally over their breakup.

"Hey, kayla and josh," i replied, easily masking what i felt in front of them with a laid back smile. Josh looked toward me, his eyes passing over me quickly.

"Where's alison?" He asked, looking back at Dawn.

"Come on, josh i dont look that much different," i scoffed, giving a slight flip of my newly curled hair.

His eyes widened.

"I swear... Wow, alison," that was all he could say his eyes fingering on me, i couldn't help but smile a little, kayla didnt noticed that much though.

"You look so pretty alison, i dont think I've ever saw you in a dress before," she teased.

"Yeah, i did...underneath my confirmation robe," i rolled my eyes, but smile wouldn't fade from my lips.

It was like a dam broke people flooded arround the estate cars where parking all over and the place, and pretty soon in a span of an hour, the place was full with people. Dawn and i were together, practically connected by our gist i felt like such a rich hostess, another one of the perks of having her for a friend she lived the high end of life.

A game of soccer had formed and i was in a daze, gazing at all the young guys running at the field kicking the checkered black and white ball. When a glass of punch was pushed into my hand, i looked up started to see dawn, her other hand was wrapped around some guys that i didn't recognised.

"Thanks," i slipped catiously, glad to realize it had been spiked yet.

"Oh... Sorry, this is Ethan. Ethan, Alison. Alison, Ethan," she introduced us, and i stuck out my hand to have it beheld in a firm hand-shake. His smile was beaming and i glanced over at Dawn at his side, who was looking at me, the question of approval in her eyes. I could see the way he held her, not possesively and he looked nice enough, so i gave a small nod. She grinned from ear to ear.

"Alison, has been my bestfriend since we started attending the same school."

He chuckled.

"So you're the famous alison brattle... You look way gorgeous to be the person Dawn explains all the time," that earned him a swift jab in the stomach by Dawn who quickly smiled at me apologetically. I just grinned.

"Lets go ethan," she said with a groan and sent me a flashed smile, mouthing."

"Sorry," she whispered

I just chuckled and looked back at the game which had paused for break now. A breeze shifted in the air, and blew my hair back, along with the rustle of trees. His hand lifted slightly off his side in a gesture. He waved once at me; i looked closely it was a man standing idle.

I lifted my own hand, fluttering at my side, to respond. But in the time it took to blink he was gone.

A warm hand caught my elbow, and i felt as if i had been burned, i looked up to meet a familar eyes.

"What are you doing here! Justin?" I gasped.

"Its a party right?" He strugged;

Releasing my hand. My cheeks flushed in embarassment as i realised, yeah it was a party, of course he could come.

"So i was invited," he continued.

"You weren't invited," i protested, but the words faded in my mouth, i knew he would be invited he was our classmate and by the way no one needed invitations, it was given.

12 THE PUSH

Walking back, i went to the pool which was mostly empty on the deep end, most of the people were playing water volleyball in the shallow water, the cheers and caws carrying over to me slightly muted. I sat down at the edge, kicking off sandles and dipping my feet into the semi-cool water. I looked down at the shimmering surface of the bottom, the way the water distorted the way the tiles lined up, kicking my feet caused a ripple affect the vision.

Slowly a figure reflected off the smoothing surface of the water, his features coming into focus. I blinked hoping he'd go away, but he stayed there, looking solemn down at the water in front of my head. Instead of speaking, he sat down next to me, slowly rolling up the hem of his jeans and taking of his shoes and socks. His feet entered the water near mine, smoothly sliding into the water with much more than mine had.

"How is your grandad now, has he got out of the hospital?" He asked, and i looked up startled, he wasn't looking at me but at Alissa and wilson. My eyes fixed curiosly on the back of his shaggy blond hair head, as he refused to look at me.

"He is getting better, it just that he can't still remember anything," I probed quietly, splashing my feet again softly, my foot going slightly too far on purpose so i could feel our feets brushing up against eachother, the cold water chilling his warm skin slightly.

"Don't worry, very soon, he will be up on his feet again stronger than he was before," he said, Now looking at me.

He smiled, he rested his hand on mine the warm was enough to make me faint, my thumb hooked arround his, without me knowing i wanted to hold more of his hand in mine, he smiled lightly, and squeezed my hand lightly, before pushing me into the pool.

I screamed, the cold water a shock as i submerged in it almost instantly my hand failed and caught on the nearest thing, which happens to be justin's legs. I tugged him in with me, hearing him yell in surprise we both crashed underneath the water, the chlorine bitting into my eyes that were caught open. I looked arround and saw justin slightly below me, his body weight taking him down farther, i swan to the surface, and broke, gasping for breath, having been taken without it suddently.

People have heard the outburst and swarmed arround the pool, Dawn was the first to reach a handout for me, and she helped me back out of the water, despite being soaked. I pulled myself the rest of the way out of the pool.

13 HIDDEN FEELINGS

June 5-7

Justin swim to the opposite side of the pool and easily lift himself out. His jeans were soaked and his T- shirt was tightened with water accenting his perfectly sculpted chest. With a groan i stood up and a towel was almost immediately wrapped around my shoulders.

My dress hung limply on me, where it once was fitting, and my bouncy curls had turned into deflated soggy mess.

Wiping the stray strand of hair out of my face i turned to go inside, Dawn close at my side.

"I hate that boy," i grumbled rushing to her room.

She helped me search for something to wear, but of course since she was looking well, she found a similar dress, but this time it was black, with a sigh, she allowed me to tie my mess of a pile of hair into a pony tail, and helped me dry off.

She insisted on retouching my make-up, me sitting to the vanity once more. I would have cry if she hadn't already scolded me so many times about smearing my macara even more with my tears.

"So...she inquired, "what have you been doing with mr justin blake lately,

Alison?" She asked innocently.

My eyebrows scrunched together,

"Nothing, we haven't been doing anything," i responded a little too quickly apparently, because her eye brows rose impeccably high on her forehead.

"Sure...What really are you doing?"

"Umm...it's just that we've been talking to each other since we were in the same for the project," uttered out suddenly.

She seemed to ponder the excuse for a moment, "well i would just about to die to have that kind of guy in my own group." She waggled her eyebrows and i rolled my eyes.

"I think he likes you though, "

"Yeah! right," i scoffed. "Sorry but that's not happening, he's a jerk -didn't you see him push me into the pool."

"But that was cute," she smiled.

"Cute! You called that cute, you're the one having to re-do all my clothing again,"

"Yeah i guess-but it's fun getting to play Barbie with a real life-size person, you cant very well decorate a Barbie's hair like yours,"

"Whatever!"

We were back down stairs an d out side by the time some of the football players were starting the bonfire. People were now slathering on bug spray to keep the pesky mosquitoes at bay, i grabbed another drink from the cooler's which had to be refilled mutiple times by the guests thirst.

Snagging myself a bottle of coke i settled against one of the bottle of coke, i settled against one of the long-logs use for sitting, near-by kayla was sitting cuddled in josh arms.

"Are you going to be okay?" Dawn whispered near me her eyes darting back at Ethan who was waiting patiently for her to return.

But here she was being the overly-friendly friend, and sacrificing her possible relationship.

I grinned. "I'll be fine, Dawn... Now go and enjoy your boyfriend,"

 She gave me a parting smile and went to snuggle up next to him. I sat there all alone taking a sip of the coke, as the music played slowly and soft, from across i could see justin leaning against another log, in a similar position as me.

I couldn't help but dream that his eyes were trained on me as the music played on.

 Sunlight shown through my eyelids making it hard to squeeze them shut enough to be enveloped in darkness. I just wanted to stay asleep...forgetting the fact that i had school today i pleaded in my mind as i groaned and turned over on the mattress so my face was buried in my pillow.

 "Alison...Alison...Are you not going to school today?" Asked diana, picking some of my clothes that was on the floor.

 Reluctantly, i stood up, muscles popped as i stretched my arms high above my head, cracking an eye i glanced at the clock and then at the open curtains on my window, that lead out into a small balcony that was always easy to just lock myself there everynight and lay under the stars as if i belonged there.

 Just another normal day, in my life, as i sat up, a wicked headache was enough to remind me that i spend all night reading and preparing for the project.

 "Good morning miss diana," i grumbled as i walked into the bathroom.

With the help of diana i got ready for school in time since i wasn't going with the school bus again, i wasn't that worried about time.

 "Alison...Alison Brattle!" Someone yelled, and i shot up in my desk. I blinked away the sleep in my eyes dazely, looking around the blurry vision, but as they focused i looked up at the concerned mr james.

 " sorry..." I mumbled, rubbing my eyes with my hands, i had fallen asleep on the warm round table in the middle of the workshop. Monday wasn't a good day for me especially the weekend after the party, that could have pratically lasted all on into sunday by the way Dawn kept dragging me from store to store at the mall, demanding that i get dresses.

 "Are you alright?" He asked, trying not to sound concerned, dusting the sawdust off my jeans, looking around at the nonchalant eyes that located me for falling asleep. I saw Justin not giving me a glance, headphones plugged into his ears as he drilled away into piece of wood, a smirk on his face, Alissa and wilson were already almost through with the hideous, electrical light they where making, that look almost like a burnt statue.

"Yeah, I'm fine... I'll just be getting back to my project," i said getting up picking up the blue prints for my entertainment center piece.

14 THE ASSIGNMENT BOOK

Mr james gave me a wary look, before doing a good thing on his part, and shrugging his shoulders and moving on his nonchalant way of lounging around the room, casually glancing at people's project. So far my group were going to make the bigger ones, being a senior, having lot of experience in here, i had a year of this class under my belt, loving the feeling of the machine under my hands, even if my vision was hampered by the annoying goggles.

Snagging my coffee cup from the table before heading to meet wilson and Alissa, even though we were grouped into two, i just wanted to see who they were making and how it works i didn't spat out the sticky sweet liquid, even if it tasted as if it had live in the freezer for a week, the tang still helped my vision focus a bit more, it was weird how sometimes you just depended on something so much, just to stay alive.

I and justin were suppose to be making our project together but i feel asleep and he didn't even bother to call me, but as i walked toward wilson and Alissa, i glanced back at justin, it had become a second nature just to glance at him every minutes despite if i wanted to or not, and i wasn't surprised to see him pulling off the look flawlessy.

I took another drink of coffee, and walked toward them, i glanced at the electrical light they were making.

"Hey, wilson," i said. With one hand on the table and the other holding my coffee cup.

"Hi, Alison, how is your project going," asked wilson, as he drilled away into a piece of wood, before i could reply him, Alissa interrupted me with her devilish words.

"Ooh...miss i know all, nobody called you here," she snapped, and i rolled my eyes, and then walked away toward justin, before she would offer another word, it was just like that was the only thing she was good at.

I strapped on the goggles they had a knack for making anyone who wore them look like a geek i starred at justin who was trying to explain some parts of the project we were making together, it was just like Mr fred knew how much i kinda hate him or not, but we both look perfectly together, i took another drink of coffee, set it down, and started the noisy sawing machine, sawdust was flying, as i carefully cut away the line i had measured over and over again to have meet the specifications that i had dsigned on my blue-print, the design process went relatively smooth, more than all the projects i had done in my former school. I glanced at justin one more time, with the smirk on his face there was no way i would fall for that.

"That's not the right way to put that, remember how i showed you before," he said. Holding my hand indicating a smaller screw on the table.

"Ooh...right, i forgot thanks," i replied.

Actually i didn't, i wasn't concentrating on the project, it was just like Mr fred knew i was going to get distracted, being around justin, that was the reason he put us together in the same group i chuckled. Shaking my head as my hand slipped on the wood, luckily not damaging the line enough that a sander couldn't easily fix. I glanced between the clock and justin's back, his arms moving slightly as he guided the piece of wood through the sander. This was going to be a very long hour.

The bell rang just as i was done clearing the sawdust off my wood, with a groan i scurried over to my table, hurrying to stash my project the room quickly cleared out, almost all of the guys in a hurry to get to lunch. Leaving justin alone with me, my wood locker was ajar so i easily whipped it open and placed my scattered starter piece into the tight space along with my neatly folded blue-print. I turned to leave that was when i heard justin called my name.

"Alison...i just want to say I'm sorry for pushing you into the pool on Saturday, i didn't mean to make you angry," he said, and i rolled my eyes.

"Its nothing, i also pushed you too into the pool, i was angry then, but not anymore," i replied with a smile.

"So... How is your grandad health now?" He asked.

I rose my eyebrow impeccably high.

"Good...he is fine, but he is still at the hospital." I replied as i stepped out into the busy hallway leaving him alone in the workshop. The school was two floors; the second floor just a couple of long hallways, split by a balcony that looked down upon the first. It remind me of the mall, the way the glass would show all the possession people were carrying beneath waist height and how the doors looked like store entrances. For a small town like this, the population in the school was amazing, all other smaller towns compiling together in the school system.

I struggled to find my locker again, in this mess of people, the number on the sliver plague on top of it was fading, with a twist of the lock and a yank of the opening mechanism the door swung open, this was definite better than the one i had in my former school, not even making me have to punch in the code half the time; but no one else knew that so i wouldn't have to worry about people trying to steal my stuffs.

I reached down for my physis II book; the home work should have been neatly pressed between the pages of chapter four with a groan i realised i left it laying on my desk, probably scattered with the rest last minutes homework, i raced to finished last night. A glance at my watch proved that i would have enough time to rush home and take much needed homework and be back before i get late for class.

It would have been much more easy, if sophine was nice to people she would have help me bring them. I snatched my keys from the top shelf and slammed the door shut, just casually walking out of the front door. There where no security cameras in the front entrance, the school wasn't really worried about vandalism the student body were relatively well behaved, but i couldn't help as if i was commiting a crime, walking out of the school in the middle of the day, earlier than normal closing hours.

"It's just because i forgot my homework book at home, I'm not doing anything wrong," i assured myself. Trying to tame myself conscience, walking across the parking lot toward the red little car that was waiting in the cooling air, then i realise there was no way i was going to drive the car home, without me getting caught, worst of all i don't want to be suspended, taking a gulp of cold air in nervousness at the filled but yet empty parking lot, time was ticking away so fast, i blinked in confusion, i checked the time again, i had twenty minutes, and a long walk to my house and back, so i started walking away from the school.

My feet trudged against the side walk, trying to walk with pulpous but inside i knew it was useless. Then a great idea came into my mind, what if i called diana and pleaded for her to bring my homework book to school for me. That's it! Why didn't i thought of this great idea before. I whipped my cellphone out. I was met with a blank black screen, as i then realised what the buzzing of it in my pocket over the past hour meant that it had died. This day is just getting better and better, i groaned.

15 THE NEW STUDENT

"What's wrong with that girl?" I asked incredulously, almost choking on the food that i had just ate. Kayla giggled, leaning into josh's side who was just smiling broadly. Dawn shrugged to finally answered,

"Tatiana...tatiana or whatever they use to call her is a trained trouble maker, she thinks she is better than everyone, because her parents are high-class fashion designers."

"Don't say that about her, she is a good girl and friendly," josh said simply. But i gave him a pointed look, as i managed to muffle the word by shovering in another forkful of salad.
I gave a small smile, and continued eating slowly, the whole lunch room just becoming a buzz in my ear, as i closed my mind of from all the conversation. But sooner or later my fork hit the plastic plate, having scraped all the last remanant of the green leaves away. The meal wasn't as big as i thought it'd be, but i sighed and started pilling all the trash from the other trays to mine.

Just as i was about to leave, Tatiana and her newly group of cronies came into the lunchroom, and sat on the seats next to us.

"Here we go again," i muttered with an eye rolled.

"Now look who is here, Chilton newly know drama queen," Dawn said almost out loud, i stood up.

"Wait...where are you going, alison?" Kayla asked. Automatically concerned, but i just shrugged.

"I don't know, maybe somewhere she's not," she starred blankly at my answer.

Its was not Like i hate tatiana but she is way worst than alissa, always behaving as if she is the only better person in the class, every minutes she bragged about owning one of the biggest estate in the states, drawing people's attention to herself. And i was getting tired of it.

"Have fun," i said as i walked away. I only briefly stopped to dump the tray of half eaten food into the trashcan, before walking out of the lunchroom doors.

I walked down the halls toward the library since i missed chemistry class i was going to study instead of staying in the lunchroom listening to tatiana lies and worst of all her stupid laugh, the large double doors that opened into the library.

The two walls that lined the doors were clear shelves that held random books that the librarians or students had recommended; behind i could make out the front desk with a woman sitting behind the computer.

The hard floor instantly turned into carpet as i stopped into the library, my feet steps muted by the softness of it, even though it wasn't exactly a soft type of carpet. A lady with her grey hair tied neatly into a tight bun on the top of her head, looked at me over the bridge of her glasses. Just a glance and she was back typing on her computer. I halted at the part of the desk near her, to neatly scrawl my name in the check in, glancing to see, she wasn't regarding me from the corner of her eyes. With a sigh i made my way over to the rows of desktop computers that were surrounding the balcony that looked down into the part of the library, with a rows of different colored binding books, barely seable from the computer desk.

I snapped on the power button and threw my books onto the counter space next to me, and i plopped down in the swivel chair, as the screen booted to life. I gave a glance around the library, not surprised to find only a few meagering souls scatterd around the large room, spread out between the shelves and desks some working on personal laptops and others just kicking back and reading books, but other occassional turn of pages and clacking of computers keys, the library was totally silent. It definitely wasnt an uncomfortable silence i had always find the library to radiate calmness, someplace i could relax, read, memorizes, and understand clearly.

The moment the internet browser appeared my hands attracted the keyboard, and my book was open to the url's i had written down for the websites we were supposed to research for the assignment. But instead my fingers flated above keys slightly drifting toward a different set of letters than i had written down. I found myself on the site to the college i had applied to, one of many, but this one was the one i had my eyes on.

I stared, glazed over at the screen that whispered possibilities of my future in my ears, teasing me with my eyes. I scanned through the page the details i had seen times without numbers. As if there would be any significant changes, but there wasn't, it was still the same amazing school that i wanted to go when I'm done with high school.

Someone cleared their throat above my head, and i jumped, my hand immediately clicking the exit button.

"Looking at something you aren't supposed to be looking?" Justin inquired, his mouth only a inches away from my ear as he whispered the word, it was just as if he had followed me all the way from the lunchroom to the library.

"No... Nothing at all, I'm researching," i stammered out, even though i had grown used to the thought of him, the very presence of his actual self set me on edge.

He smiled, sitting down next to me, picking up the cover of the book.

"Yeah, that looked like chemical formula of -- atomic structure and shape," he dropped the book, and i rolled my eyes vaguely, clickling the internet search back on again, the clean homepage popping up.

"For a girl like you so...serious with her studies," he scoffed. Can i explain today chemistry lesson you misse?"

"Hmm...don't tell me you followed me all the way, just to explain it to me," i said.

"Is that exactly how it looks like?" He asked.

"Well...you shouldn't be bodering yourself over someone else problem," i said, simply typing in the website.

16 THE TROUBLE MAKER

"What's wrong with that girl?" I asked incredulously, almost choking on the food that i had just ate. Kayla giggled, leaning into josh's side who was just smiling broadly. Dawn shrugged to finally answered,

"Tatiana...tatiana or whatever they use to call her is a trained trouble maker, she thinks she is better than everyone, because her parents are high-class fashion designers."

"Don't say that about her, she is a good girl and friendly," josh said simply. But i gave him a pointed look, as i managed to muffle the word by shovering in another forkful of salad.
I gave a small smile, and continued eating slowly, the whole lunch room just becoming a buzz in my ear, as i closed my mind of from all the conversation. But sooner or later my fork hit the plastic plate, having scraped all the last remanant of the green leaves away. The meal wasn't as big as i thought it'd be, but i sighed and started pilling all the trash from the other trays to mine.

Just as i was about to leave, Tatiana and her newly group of cronies came into the lunchroom, and sat on the seats next to us.

"Here we go again," i muttered with an eye rolled.

"Now look who is here, Chilton newly know drama queen," Dawn said almost out loud, i stood up.

"Wait...where are you going, alison?" Kayla asked. Automatically concerned, but i just shrugged.

"I don't know, maybe somewhere she's not," she starred blankly at my answer.

Its was not Like i hate tatiana but she is way worst than alissa, always behaving as if she is the only better person in the class, every minutes she bragged about owning one of the biggest estate in the states, drawing people's attention to herself. And i was getting tired of it.

"Have fun," i said as i walked away. I only briefly stopped to dump the tray of half eaten food into the trashcan, before walking out of the lunchroom doors.

I walked down the halls toward the library since i missed chemistry class i was going to study instead of staying in the lunchroom listening to tatiana lies and worst of all her stupid laugh, the large double doors that opened into the library.

The two walls that lined the doors were clear shelves that held random books that the librarians or students had recommended; behind i could make out the front desk with a woman sitting behind the computer.

The hard floor instantly turned into carpet as i stopped into the library, my feet steps muted by the softness of it, even though it wasn't exactly a soft type of carpet. A lady with her grey hair tied neatly into a tight bun on the top of her head, looked at me over the bridge of her glasses. Just a glance and she was back typing on her computer. I halted at the part of the desk near her, to neatly scrawl my name in the check in, glancing to see, she wasn't regarding me from the corner of her eyes. With a sigh i made my way over to the rows of desktop computers that were surrounding the balcony that looked down into the part of the library, with a rows of different colored binding books, barely seable from the computer desk.

I snapped on the power button and threw my books onto the counter space next to me, and i plopped down in the swivel chair, as the screen booted to life. I gave a glance around the library, not surprised to find only a few meagering souls scatterd around the large room, spread out between the shelves and desks some working on personal laptops and others just kicking back and reading books, but other occassional turn of pages and clacking of computers keys, the library was totally silent. It definitely wasnt an uncomfortable silence i had always find the library to radiate calmness, someplace i could relax, read, memorizes, and understand clearly.

The moment the internet browser appeared my hands attracted the keyboard, and my book was open to the url's i had written down for the websites we were supposed to research for the assignment. But instead my fingers flated above keys slightly drifting toward a different set of letters than i had written down. I found myself on the site to the college i had applied to, one of many, but this one was the one i had my eyes on.

I stared, glazed over at the screen that whispered possibilities of my future in my ears, teasing me with my eyes. I scanned through the page the details i had seen times without numbers. As if there would be any significant changes, but there wasn't, it was still the same amazing school that i wanted to go when I'm done with high school.

Someone cleared their throat above my head, and i jumped, my hand immediately clicking the exit button.

"Looking at something you aren't supposed to be looking?" Justin inquired, his mouth only a inches away from my ear as he whispered the word, it was just as if he had followed me all the way from the lunchroom to the library.

"No... Nothing at all, I'm researching," i stammered out, even though i had grown used to the thought of him, the very presence of his actual self set me on edge.

He smiled, sitting down next to me, picking up the cover of the book.

"Yeah, that looked like chemical formula of -- atomic structure and shape," he dropped the book, and i rolled my eyes vaguely, clickling the internet search back on again, the clean homepage popping up.

"For a girl like you so...serious with her studies," he scoffed. Can i explain today chemistry lesson you misse?"

"Hmm...don't tell me you followed me all the way, just to explain it to me," i said.

"Is that exactly how it looks like?" He asked.

"Well...you shouldn't be bodering yourself over someone else problem," i said, simply typing in the website.

17 THE FRIENDLY ENEMY

He smiled devishly. "Do you know what makes it so much fun," he winked at me and i realised i had made a mistake of words.

"And anyway, you arent really all that much of a stranger, we've been friends remember?"

I whipped around, "we. Are. Not." I whispered so low that it was almost the same as thinking.

He smirked. "Well we are friends, i dont know if you are implying something further," he raised an eyebrow expectantly. My eyes squinted and my face felt as hot as a curling iron, surely the color of a tomato, in embarrasment.

"Nevermind, leave me to do my work," i growled swiveling back towards the computer screen. I had been hoping that what Dawn have been telling me to turn out not to be true, but she was right anyway, i growled.

He thought, his finger tapping dramatically on the desk to emphasize the sarcasm that was sure to come.

"Nah, i think i prefer sitting here with you, annoying you," he smiled. I groaned, but started with the sites, this was going to be a long couple hours.

My research time in the library with justin chatting up in an annoying manner, leaning over my shoulder and honestly making me on nerves end. By the end of the second website i had taken notes on, i was ready to rip my hair out or no... I'd rather rip his hair out instead.

Just then tatiana walked in, but this time she was not with her cronies. My smiling face turned into frowning face, as I saw her walking toward my direction.

"Hi...alison," she said.

"Hey..." I replied and my hands tensed around the mouse.

She walked toward justin with a misty smile on her face.

"Hi... Justin," she murmured. "Can you please help me with today's explanation of chemisty lesson, I don't really umderstand."

I gave a glanced toward them and then continued with what I was doing. The bell rang on time, but yet all to soon, and I snatched my stack of books, the computer promptly turning off behind me.

"Sorry...tatiana but I can't now later we will talk about it," I heard justin telling tatiana, as he walked leisurely next to me. with a groan tatiana walked down the stairs.

"Don't tell me you left Tatiana all alone in the library, when she really need your help, because you want to follow me," I said as we walked down the stairs.

"No...its just that I'm not ready now to explain anything to anyone," he smiled, while I headed down the hall. I was rolling my eyes so much when he spoke that I was sure they would just rolled away.

"Well, since I'm through with the library, good-bye," I said simply and turned the opposite direction.

"Wait." He said, and I paused, turning around, waiting for the punch line.

"After school, can you go out with me?" He asked. "I'll be very happy if you will say yes," he tapered off, with a cough into his hand, before his face fell back to his normal cocky self.

I considered it for a moment, and then decided that I rather not have him there, his presence rather intimidating, while I did my homework.

"Sorry, I got things to do later, like taking care of my grandma and grandpa," I lied. Actually my grandad was still at the hospital but according to the doctor, he will be ready to come home with us, when he has fully recovered. I side stepped away leaving him standing there in the middle of the hallway, people swerving around him to get to class before the bell announced them late. I heard him sigh disappointed.

After I submit my chemistry assignment, and now it was closing hour, I took the brisk walk to the sidewalks. Almost forgetting that I didn't have a warm car to take me home, since I didn't come to school with my car.

As I walked down the street I began to feel the effects of justin, as if his arms were wrapped around mine, keeping me warm in the cold.

"Great, he is bordering me, even when he i'snt around," i muttered, with an eye rolled.

"Hey, you need a ride?" A voice called out, and I turned my head, to see a black covertible car, and Justin smiling at me. I grinned back, and then shake my head to indicate no, even when that was what I need most at that time.

"Come on, you know your house is still far are you to trek all the way home," he said. With a smirk on his face.

"Yes, I could use a ride, thank you, stranger," I replied, walking around the passengers seat I pulled expectanctly on the handle, and found it locked; I knocked on the window to get his attention, he grinned widely, but eventually hit the unlock button.

"Well thats just fine, you offer me a ride and don't actually give it," I huffed, but smiling thankfully.

"You look good, when you smile," he replied.

"Okay," I muttered, and we both laughed.

"So am I dropping you off at home?" He asked as we where nearing the road to my neighbourhood.

"Yes..." I replied. He stared straight into my eyes, a soft light behind the silver irises.

"Alison, there is something I wanted to ask you," he said.

"What is that this time?" I asked. Bitting my lip, waiting to hear what he wanted to say.

"Please don't say no," he muttered. "You are very intelligent and beautiful girl, I have ever met, I have always wanted to say this but don't know how to."

I starred at him, like someone who had been hypnotize, waiting to hear his final words.

"Alison... Will you be my girlfriend?" He asked, and reached across the armrests, only to briefly gasp my hand long enough to give my fingers a reasuring squeeze.

"Hmm...huh," I grumbled. Starring into his eyes I could see he was somehow almost disappointed.

"Yes," I whispered.

18 COMPLETE LIAR

The next day, I walked into the class a minute late, having stop by to check on dawn but she already left, I walked toward my seat and sat down quietly. Mrs Eleanor walked in some minutes later but the look on her face wasn't friendly at all.

"Alison...bring your bag and books, I want to check them," she said.

I snatched my backpack and books from the desk walked toward the front of the class and gave it to her.

"Today, someone placed an anonymous message in my mailbox claming you stole the text answers," mrs Eleanor said as she searched my bag, not quite long she brought out the a white paper with letters written on it.

"And it looks like the anonymous person was right."

"What!" The whole class shouted.

I gave a confused look. "But that's not true, someone placed that piece of paper in my bag," I said.

"But you answered all the questions correctly," she replied.

"I did...?" I said surprised. "Yes, thats because I study hard for it."

"Mrs Eleanor, Alison, always score high on your test ever since she came to this school," Dawn said, in my defence.

"This so like you, Alison, you're usually so well behaved," said tatiana, and everybody turned toward her direction.

"Oh...of course you put the answers in my bag, you're the anonymous informal," I shouted pointing at tatiana, but I was not sure she was the one, but anyone who did such thing hate me so much.

"You can't accuse someone, alison without prove," mr eleanor said, more angry than i had ever seen her be since I came to the school.

"But...but I'm sure its her, she stole the test answers and put it in my bag," I replied, almost in tears.

"Thats impossible alison, tatiana wasn't around when we wrote that test, she hasn't even got enrolled then," mrs Eleanor said.

"Excuse me, Mrs eleanor but everyone knows that is not like Alison to cheat, she study so hard even in the library," commented justin. So as the rest of the class trying to defend me, and now the class was noisy.

"Alison,Tatiana, please go to the principal office till we get to the bottom of this," Mrs eleanor said, and once more the class was back to its normal silent, as we both walked out the door.

As we walked Down the hallway toward the principal office there was a smirk on tatiana's face.

"I swear I'll make your life unbearable Alison-let's see how you get out of this one," she said.

"I'm not falling in your trap, tatiana, and by the way what's you're reason by doing all this what will you gain from all this?" I asked.

We got to the door of the principal office but instead Tatiana walked away toward one of the stairs.

"Where are you going?" I asked.

She smiled. "You are about to find out," she replied walking down the stairs, when she got to the end of the stairs she sat down on the floor and started screaming holding her legs.

"Ouch...ouch...ah...ah, my legs," she cried.

I stood there with my mouth opened, in surprise, when people heard her screaming the rushed out to check what was happening.

"What happened!" Mr maxwell asked as he opened the door.

"Alison...oh...pushed me down the stairs," she cried.

"Alison, get in my office now," mr Maxwell said angrily.

I sat down on a chair in the principal office, and watched her crying saying alot of things, which I did not do.

"I don't know, why Alison did not like me, I tried so much to be her friend," she cried. "But she keeps calling me a lier, a trouble maker trying to make everyone hates me."

"Sir, it wasn't me I didn't do anything, I don't know Any of all she is saying," I said.

"After all that, she is pushing me down the stairs...oh oh, Alison want to kill me," she cried. Holding her knee.

"Those are totally lies!" I shouted.

"Go on, tatiana," mr maxwell said. Ignoring all my words, giving tatiana enough space to lie more.

"She even, told me that I will suffer for taking her seat, apart from that...oh oh she...stole my necklace, the one I got from my grandmother, a heart shape mendant," she said.

That was when I stood up, I was angry now, very angry.

"Thats not true I did not do any of what she is saying I did, I don't even know how her necklace looks like!" I shouted.

"See, she's even shouting at me now, if you where not here, she would have beat me up," she cried.

"Do you have prove, on all what you are telling me that Alison did?" Mr maxwell asked.

"Hmm...I have prove," she replied. Immediately we all walked down the stairs toward my locker where she said I had put the necklace.

"Alison...open your locker," mr maxwell said. I opened it to my horror, a blue colored necklace fell down, she picked it up.

"Uuh...my necklace," she gasped.

I couldn't believe what I was seeing, I have never stole anything in my life before, and only I knew the code to open my locker. Everyone was angry now even Dawn and everyone who had tried their best to defend me.

"I swear, I didn't do anything, she is making up all this whole thing, you know tatiana is lying don't you, justin," I said trying to defend myself feeling helpless.

"Mr maxwell, please I know...Alison didn't do it," commented justin, but mr maxwell shouted. "Enough" no one said anything again.

"Alison brattle you are expelled from this school, wait your grandma is coming to take you home, I have already informed her.

"You are so heartless, Alison," kayla said as they all left leaving me alone. In tears I I started parking my books into my bag.

19 THE BAD DAY

August 5

By the time my grandmother arrived at my school i was already done packing my books into my bag and was now standing at the entrance of the school, she came down of the car being assisted by diana. I couldn't wait for her to reach where I was standing before rushing toward where she was and i hug her.

"Alison we heard what happened, did you do such thing?" asked diana.

"No...i know she can't do such thing," replied grandma, defending me.

Diana collected my backpack, from me as we entered the car, I wasn't happy at all, the worst thing of all was that all my plans to study in a college after highschool was over, the worst that could happened now is that my parents will have to put me in another school, I will miss my grandparents and all my friends at chilton high.

I stared at people passing by through the car window just like I did when I was coming to my grandparents place. Even though if I got enrolled in another school I have to wait till another year again.

Now tears were streaming down my cheeks as I sat next to grandma.

"Don't worry, Alison evetything will be alright," diana said.

But all what was on my mind was, why will tatiana do such thing just to get me expelled? I mean what was her reason.

"Alison...she may have no reason, maybe she is just jealous of something you have that she don't have," replied diana.

That was when I realise that all what I was thinking about I was saying it out loud in the car. By the time we got home that day it was already raining. I assisted diana in all her chores and now I was very tired.

We sat and ate dinner in silence that evening with the look on my grand mother face I sure knew she wasn't happy at all, its not like her to be silent the way she was that evening or maybe she was trying to hide how terribly sad she was.

After dinner I helped Diana washed all the dishes even though the dishwasher was working fine I insisted on washing it.

As I was about going to my room, I heard a knock on the door. I walked to the door and opened it.

"Alison...oh I've really missed you," dawn said almost screaming, we wrapped eachother in an intense bear hug.

"Oh...come in sis," I said. And we both laughed.

"Don't worry Alison, that witch tatiana will soon be exposed and you will come back to school," dawn said with an assuring smile.

I just smiled back at her, knowing the fact that I won't go back to chilton, but I wasn't going to tell her, i don't want her hope to be for nothing.

We talked and laughed till it was time for her to go home, even though I persuaded her to spend a night at with me, she insisted that she didn't informed her parents about it.

I followed dawn to the door and then wave goodbye to her.

I don't realise how much time has passed until the sound of my dad's car sends me into a panic. Scooping up the dripping, I race to my bedroom wondering what my dad would have to say.

"I...need to pray...I need to pray," I whispered to myself.

"Whats going on?" Dad suddenly behind me, standing in the door way that has no door.

Down on my knees at my bedside, I turn to dad with all innocence I can muster and fold my hands.

"Just saying a few prayers, " I replied as we hugged eachother.

My Dad eyes bug out in surprise. " since when do you pray?"

"Since I thought we might need some help,"

"I can't disagree," Dad grunts. He starts to leave, but turn back to say.

"Could you maybe put in a plug for my work and your gandad's while you're at it?"

"Dad..." I called out. "Is there anything going on over there, that I don't know about, please tell me."

"Its nothing..." He replied.

Dad rarely lets on when something's bothering him, so I figure things must really be serious.

"Let me see what I can do," I said. And he goes, I actually do muttered a quick prayer, in case someone's listening.

20 THE WORST DAY

August 14

Forget about the day I got expelled from school, or the day my grandad had an accident. Forget about the new year day when all this started the fourteenth day of august- wednessday, august 14- is the worst day...OF MY ENTIRE LIFE!!!!!

And guess what? The worst day for the brattle's family.

As usual I woke up, eat breakfast, take my bath, since I wasn't going to school I helped diana in some of the chores, when dad was ready to go to work I hugged him and waved bye, as I watched his car drove off the parking lots. Through the window I can see the grey sky getting cloudier at the minutes, I review my notes I actually fell asleep while I was reading.

The ringing tone of my phone woke me up, that was when I realise I had been sleeping I quickly gave a glance at the clock beside my bed_ 1:45pm.

"Hello..." I answered.

But all I could hear was the voice of diana crying, my breath caught in my throat, and in that moment I was trying to figure out what was wrong I tried asking over and all over again but she couldn't tell me, I ran down the stairs almost stepped on fluffy who was busy sleeping. But no one was at home I was the only one, I tried calling diana again she couldn't pick, when she finally did it was in the evening after I had almost fainted thinking and imagining all sorts of things.

And then there I was standing at the entrance waiting as the car drove in, as usual diana assisted my grandmother down to her room, she was quiet and wasn't happy at all.

I followed them to the room the first indication that something was wrong is that my grandmother didnt say anything she won't look me in the face. Even diana tears rolled down from her eyes every second.

"Whats wrong?" I look from face to face, trying to figure out what was wrong, but no one said anything, I kissed grandma on her cheek as she lay on her bed i notice she was crying too.

I followed diana to the kitchen almost as sad as they were I wanted to cry I was thinking hard and my heart beating fast.

"Please, Mrs diana tell me whats wrong...what happened?" I asked now as tears rolled down my cheek as if o knew what was coming.

"Alison...We lost your grandad," she replied. What I heard makes all the blood in my body rush to my feet, and I have to grab hold of the kitchen counter to keep me from collapsing.

"We received a calm this morning from the hospital, they said early this morning his temperature rises and before they would do anything to save his life it was too late," she continued.

"Oh my God!" I muttered as tears rolled down my eyes.

"You're grandad died of heart cancer," Diana said, Before walking out of the kitchen.

I gasped my father never told me things where this serious, but then he never really tells me the bad stuff. Suddenly I feel sicker and sadder and worst than I had ever felt.

Even worst than when I was expelled from school. To keep me from crying again I bite inside of my cheek until I could taste blood in my mouth I walked up the stairs to my room. I couldn't believe this, everyone hid it as a secret from me and now I've lost my grandad the favourite of all, I wanted to call my dad but I couldn't.

I laid down on my bed, each time I remembered my grandad I cried so hard, I picked up my phone from the bed I was going to call my dad but my vision was blurred by tears. Finally I got it right, the phone kept on ringing I tried calling my mum but her phone was switched off.

I lay my head on the pillow and sob. If only there were somebody I could talk to, I think. But who is there to tell? Not Dad. Not Dawn or justin. Mum line was off. And this was even more hard and painful for grandma.

Now. I am totally...completely...hopelessly alone in the world.

21 THE RETURN

August 15-16

I stood up from my bed and walked toward the window, I could remember each words, every memories of my grandad how he use to tell me stories of when he was very young and a lot more, how much this was like a tragedy, just then I heard my phone ringing I reluctantly walked toward my beside and snatched the phone from the table.

My cellphone goes on. Its justin.

"Hello," I said as I sat on the bed.

"Hi...Alison," justin starts in. "I'm sorry for your loss, dawn told me all what happened, I hope you're fine."

"Yeah...I am, but I don't think my grandma is feeling that much in the same way," I replied trying to open to him.

"Don't worry alison very soon everything will be alright, but ensure you take good care of your grandma," he continued.

"I will," I replied.

"Alison...I heard something today at school, that I think might be helpful to you," justin said.

Just then, I heard dad come through the front door. I my closet and said.

"I gotta go," as I snap the phone shut.

"Alison..." Dad called. "How was your day? I couldn't reply instead I rushed and hugged him.

"Dad my day hadn't been good at all," I replied.

My dad walked into my bedroom and we sat on the bed, I tried to hid the tears in my eyes I didn't want my dad to start getting worried after the death of his father was more heart break to him, but however he noticed.

"My treasure, wipe those tears away, I know its hard for all of us but I don't want to ever see you cry again," he said.

"I smile sweetly, when I was small anytime I had a hard time at school my dad will always tell me that I shouldn't cry about those things bordering me that he is always there for me, my mum will then winked at me i n a funny way. Will end up laughing, and now hearing dad's voice telling me to wipe my tears was the most amazing thing ever.

"Guess what sweetie...?

I smiled. "What!

"Mr maxwel called me this morning he said you can be coming to school as from tomorrow so you can graduate with your mate," he replied.

I wasn't surprise but I was expecting it because I knew I was innocent and that wicked tatiana was just making up those stories to get me expelled I didn't border to ask the reason but I was happy.

That night we eat mac 'n' cheese without saying a word grandma couldn't come to the dinning room to eat with us so diana took her dinner to her room. After I watched diana giving grandma her seven-fourty pills, I hangout in my bedroom, pretending to read, but my gaze keeps drifting to my grandad. I'm so distracted that when my mum pops in just before bedtime and say.

"Don't forget..." I jump about three feets out of my chair.

"Jeez!" I yelped.

"Sorry," Mum says. "Don't mean to scare you my baby girl," she smiled and walked in she sat next to me took one of the textbook I was reading.

"I heard you are going to school tomorrow I know you are happy, but I want you to know one thing and never forget this you are special to me and your dad, and we are always here for you, I have another good news...guess what my princess!"

"What?" I asked.

"Remember how you use to feel lonely when I and your dad were not around, you would always tell me you wish you had a sibling to talk to, play with when you were small," mum continued. "Now your wishes have come true,"

"Mum...are you pregnant?" I asked with a smile on my face.

"Yes! Mum replied.

The death of my grandad was a shock to everyone even I, but when I heard that my mom was pregnant and my finally I will have a brother or sister to talk to I was so happy that I almost forgot about how sad I was about my grandad death.

The next morning I shuffle around the apartment, burping a lot and bumping into walls, I'm still half asleep I got dressed for school and now was in the kitchen. I was eating my cereal over the kitchen sink when my dad walked past on his way out.

"Have a blessed day, my treasure," he called over his shoulder, but he didnt wait for an answer or for my morning greeting.

Dumping the cereal bowl in the sink I walked Into the living room took my bag from the couch and walked toward the door. I closed the door gently behind me since sophine was no longer around, the house was so quiet no one to play loud music disturbing our next door neighbours, goodnews she finally went to live with her parents.

Two minutes to nine from across the street I drove my car on full speed, when I got to school I was almost late for physis class I walked to where my locker was, I packed my books from my bag into the locker one after the other when I was done I walked toward the library.

"--you're kidding me," I said. My mouth agape at the mess that use to be the library. The giant picture window that opened out to the back of the school was cracked and shaltered in places. The doors were barricaded from people walking much further than the front desk, because it still looked as if it would shatter into a million pieces over the rest of the library and books there was police around the breakage, carefully stepping around the glass shards that had already been knocked out of place onto the carpet. Quiet commotion from them as they investigated the problem throughly. But just as there was a small crowd down there, there was a large crowd pushing against the barricade of the doors I was smooshed between a girl with an extremely oversized bag at her side that was jabbing me in my ribs with a pencil of some sort and the wall which was equally unforgiving. But atleast I had a good veiw of the remains of the library that only minutes earlier.

I sighed, and with a roll of my eyes, I tried pushing backwards out of the crowd. The moment I pushed past the last person I could suddenly breathe again and move more importanly. A glance at the overhead clock confirmed that i still had a good half hour before the first bell would ring.

The halls were not as full as usual, all the normal traffic heading in the direction of the library, except for the few bored souls who really didn't care, and rather just wander the halls.

I walked up the stairs, more than steps off the stairs I came to a rest in front of justin who was opening his locker. My heart faltered and nearly stopped. I know he asked me to be his girlfriend which I accepted but when I got expelled we stop seeing each other, even though he use to call me almost three times a day when I was at home I was still missing his face.

"Hey,"

I said the simplest word very softly, having to keep it so low so it wouldn't croak and crack; having it soft was less embarrassing. I stood there awkwardly by his locker as he didnt bother to look up for a second, picking up his chemistry book off the bottom of his locker, when he did look up though those crystal sliver eyes regarded me blankly for moment.

"Good morning, I'm so happy to see you back in school again," he said.

"Yeah, and same here," I replied. As we both stared at eachother, with his hand almost touching mine my smile faltered but I sighed, I reached out and snatched at his arm.

"Can you pick me up tomorrow for school?" I asked randomly, my face feeling as if sun burnt in embarrassment. His eyebrows furrowed but he nodded, and then smiled.

"Yeah...umm, sure. I'd get to class if I were you, its getting
Late," he shuttered out, but quickly regained his composure and disappeared into the swarm. I glanced at the clock again, twenty whole minutes until the the bell would go off, but some reason, I still headed to my first hour.

"I can't believe someone would throw a brick at the library...Dawm muttered, as she walked with me towards the back doors of the school out towards her car. I clutched my book tightly to my chest, my mind reeling over the library incident.

"Umm... What about tatiana, I havent seen her since I came to school?" I asked pretending to care.

"She got suspended after justin told mr maxwell all what he heard telling her friends, even when she was called to the office she said it with her mouth that she was jealous of your intelligence and didn't want you around Justin," replied Dawn.

Actually I didn't know what to say I was just speechless, I was happy everyone know the kind of person she is, but I was ready to forgive her as long as she changes.

I waved vigorously as I watched dawn entered her car and drove off, I turned toward my car and then sighed.

"Wait..." Justin said his voice almost silent, a whisper. I turned around and he smiled he seem happy.

"I need to ask you one thing, can you do a favour for me?" He asked, his voice caught as if he was going against himself, his conscience, a dilemma I found myself in frequently.

"Sure, I guess...is it going to be something I regrets?" I teased back, bringing back his words from earlier he smiled vaguely.

"Will you go out with me today?" He asked walking close to me.

"Yes!" I replied.

Even though I wasn't happy when my parents told me to spend the holiday with my grandparents, I figure out that sometimes spending time with your family is the best thing ever, this is one of the holiday that I won't ever forget.

The end.

ABOUT THE AUTHOR

Clara joel is an author of teenfiction for both adults and teens, including for the whole family and her upcoming novel "things i remember" will be one of the best you've ever read, She's Too Pretty to Burn. She was born in nigeria, she stays with her parents in lagos, she a student in the university of benin. When not writing, she can be found reading her books making research on biology and other science subjects, despite the fact that she is a science student her love for writing was never omitted, she started writing at the age of twelve and have written many books

You can chat with clara on Twitter or Instagram at

Instagram :@clarajoel88

Facebook: clara Joel

Twitter: clara joel 1